Katie Woo

Loves School

by Fran Manushkin
illustrated by Tammie Lyon

capstone

Katie Woo is published by Picture Window Books
A Capstone Imprint
1710 Roe Crest Drive
North Mankato, MN 56003
www.capstonepub.com

Library of Congress Cataloging-in-Publication Data
Manushkin, Fran.
  Katie Woo loves school / by Fran Manushkin ; illustrated by Tammie Lyon.
       p. cm. — (Katie Woo)
  Summary: Combines four previously published stories, including Moo, Katie Woo!, Make believe class, Katie finds a job, and Who needs glasses, in which Katie and her friends participate in school activities.
  ISBN 978-1-4795-2027-5 (pbk.)
  ISBN 978-1-4795-5654-0 (ebook)
1. Woo, Katie (Fictitious character)—Juvenile fiction. 2. Elementary schools—Juvenile fiction. 3. Chinese Americans--Juvenile fiction. [1. Elementary schools—Fiction. 2. Schools—Fiction. 3. Chinese Americans—Fiction.] I. Lyon, Tammie, ill. II. Title. III. Series: Manushkin, Fran. Katie Woo.
  PZ7.M3195Kbi 2013
  813.54—dc23
                                                    2012049914

Photo Credits
Greg Holch, pg. 96; Tammie Lyon, pg. 96

Designer: Kristi Carlson

Printed and bound in the USA.
052017   010512R

Table of Contents

Make-Believe Class

It was a cold gray day.

Miss Winkle told her class, "Let's make up a story together. It will help us forget this winter day."

Katie raised her hand.

"I have an idea!" she said. "Let's pretend our school is in a warm, sunny place."

Miss Winkle smiled. "Let's put our school on an island," she said.

"Great!" said Pedro. "We will get there on a sailboat instead of a bus!"

"But how will we do our math?" asked Miss Winkle.

"I know!" JoJo said. "We will add up the seagulls when they land."

"And subtract them when they fly away," said Katie.

"We can't write on paper," said
Miss Winkle. "The wind will blow it
away."

"I know!" said JoJo. "We can write
in the wet sand."

"We won't need erasers," said Katie. "The sea will take away our mistakes."

"I want to go to school in
Australia!" shouted Peter. "It's upside
down there."

"That is only on the globe," said Miss Winkle. "It's not really upside down."

"Good!" said Susie. "I would get so dizzy!"

"Let's go to school on the moon!"
yelled Chuck. "It would be so cool!"

"We can draw pictures of the Earth floating in space," said JoJo. "It's a good science lesson!"

"And a great art lesson too!" said Miss Winkle.

"Gym class would be the best!"
said Katie. "On the earth, I can't jump
high. But on the moon, I could fly!"

"But the moon is so gray," said Pedro. "I would miss the nice green earth."

"Let's ride our rocket back, and land in the sea!" said Miss Winkle. "We will study the fish underwater."

"Sea turtles are neat too!" shouted Chuck.

"Sharks are not," warned Susie. "Let's sail back to land."

"I agree," said JoJo. "I want to see Washington, D.C."

"We can have our class at the U.S. Mint," said Miss Winkle. "That's where they make all our money."

Katie joked, "Math class would last forever! There is so much money to count!"

"Look!" Miss Winkle pointed out the window. "It's snowing! The first snow of the year!"

"I want to stay here!" said Katie.
"There is no snow on a warm island."

"Or on the moon!" yelled JoJo.

"And you can't make snowballs in
the sea," added Pedro. "Or at the U.S.
Mint."

"I think it snows in Australia,"
said Miss Winkle. "But I am not sure."

"I am sure about one thing,"
said Katie. "Miss Winkle is a terrific
teacher! She turned a gray day into a
happy one!"

"Hooray for Miss Winkle!" everyone shouted.

Then the recess bell rang, and they all went out to play.

Katie Finds
a Job

"I have to find a job," Katie told her mom.

"There's no hurry," her mom said. "You have years to think about it."

"I don't," sighed Katie. "I need a
job by Friday. We are having Career
Day at school. I need to talk about the
job I want when I grow up."

Katie asked the bus driver, "Do you like driving a bus?"

"Yes!" the driver said.

"I might like it, too," said Katie. "Can I try driving?"

"I don't think so," the driver said. "You're too young."

Pedro's dad worked
at a bank.

"I like money," said
Katie. "But I don't want
to add and subtract all day."

Pedro's mom said, "Taking care of a
new baby is a big job."

"That's for sure," Katie agreed.
"I'm not ready to be a mom!"

"I like being a chef," said Katie's mom.

"I like to eat," Katie said. "But I don't want to cook all day."

The next day at school, JoJo said, "I love the sea and whales. My job will be teaching people about them. But how can I do a great Career Day talk on whales?"

"I know how!" said Katie. "We will make a giant whale, and you can play a CD of their songs. My dad has one at home."

"That's terrific!" said JoJo.

"I'm going to
be a geologist,"
said Pedro. "I'm

bringing lots of rocks for my talk."

Katie shook her head. "Pedro, you
need more than a pile of rocks."

"I have an idea," Katie said. "Let's make a volcano."

She found a book that showed how to do it.

"Wow!" shouted Pedro. "My talk will be terrific!"

But Katie still did not have a job.
"I can't decide," she said. "I love to
do a little bit of everything."

Finally, it was Career Day.

JoJo's talk was splendid.

"Your whale songs added so much," said Miss Winkle.

Pedro's volcano was exciting! "Well done!" said Miss Winkle.

The whole class clapped and cheered.

"Katie," said Miss Winkle, "it's time to tell us about your job."

Katie stood up. "I'm sorry," she said. "But I couldn't find one." She sat down again, looking sad.

"Wait a minute!" said Pedro. "Katie
did a great job helping me. She showed
me how to build a volcano!"

"Katie helped me, too," said JoJo.
"She gave me terrific ideas! Katie's
good at telling people what to do."

"That's it!" Katie told Miss Winkle. "I'll be the person who tells people what to do! Is that a job?"

"It is," said Miss
Winkle. "People who
solve problems are
called leaders."

"I'm a leader!"
said Katie proudly. "I'll go around the
world and fix every problem!"

"That's a big job," Miss Winkle said. "Why don't you start with something smaller?"

"Okay," decided Katie, "I'll just be the president of the United States."

"Well," said Miss Winkle, "that's a big job, too. But if anyone can do it, it's you, Katie Woo!"

Who Needs Glasses?

"Today's class is about dinosaurs," said Miss Winkle. "This dinosaur is called Sue. It was named after the lady who found the bones."

"Cool!" said Katie.

Miss Winkle asked Pedro to read to the class. "I can't," he said. "My book is blurry."

"It's not," said Miss Winkle. "I think you need to get your eyes checked."

A few days later, Pedro showed
Katie his new glasses.

"I feel a little weird," said Pedro.

"You look great!" said Katie.

"Today," said Miss Winkle, "we are making dinosaur dioramas. You will work in teams of three."

"Let's be a team," Katie told Pedro and JoJo. They began to work.

"Where are your glasses?" Katie asked Pedro.

"Um . . . I think I lost them," Pedro said.

Pedro began to read from his
book. "Most dinosaurs ate pants."

"No!" said Katie, laughing. "Not
pants — plants!"

"Oh! Right!" said Pedro.

Pedro read another dinosaur fact: "The word 'dinosaur' means terrible blizzard."

"No!" Katie told him. "It's terrible lizard!"

"I'd better read the facts," Katie told Pedro. "You can start making our diorama."

"Great!" Pedro said. "I love to draw!"

Pedro drew a dinosaur.

"That looks like my cat," said

Barry, the new boy.

Pedro squinted at his drawing.

Katie told him, "I wish you could find

your glasses."

During recess, Katie got an idea.
She came back to class without her
glasses.

"Where are they?" asked Pedro.

"I don't know," said Katie. "But I
don't really need them."

Katie sat down.

"Watch out!" warned JoJo.
"You are sitting on the clay for our
diorama."

"Oops!" said Katie. "I didn't see
that."

"I can make a paper dinosaur," said Katie. She squinted as she folded the paper.

"That looks like a boat," said Barry. "Your team is very funny!"

"I don't think so," sighed JoJo.

"Our project is a mess!" said Katie. "And we are running out of time. If only I could find my glasses, then I could see!"

"Look!" said Pedro suddenly. "I found mine! They were in my pocket the whole time!"

Pedro began to work. He made a
terrific clay dinosaur, and he painted a
scary volcano.

"Looking good!" cheered Katie and
JoJo.

"Very good!" agreed Barry.

"Hey!" said Katie. "Guess what? I found my glasses, too. They were in my pocket the whole time, too!"

Pedro laughed. "Katie, you are very tricky!"

"Maybe," said Katie.

She laughed too.

JoJo told Pedro, "You look smart in your glasses."

"I feel smart," he said, admiring his work.

Miss Winkle admired it too.

She took photos of all the teams
and their projects.

Katie and Pedro and JoJo smiled
proudly.

"You look terrific!" Miss Winkle
said.

And they did!

Moo,
Katie Woo!

One day, Miss Winkle asked the class, "Where do eggs and milk come from?"

"From the store," said Katie Woo.

"That's true," said Miss Winkle. "But before that, they came from chickens and cows."

"I'd like to see those chickens and cows," said Katie.

"Me too," yelled JoJo.

"Me three!" joked Pedro.

"You will," said Miss Winkle.

"Tomorrow we are going to a farm."

The class rode a bus to the farm. When they got there, Farmer Jordan showed Katie how to milk a cow.

"Moo!" said the cow.

"Moo to you!" joked Katie Woo.

"Now let's visit the chickens," said Miss Winkle.

The chicks were cheeping, the roosters were crowing, and the hens were laying eggs.

Pedro joked, "If these eggs fall
down, they will be scrambled eggs."

"Yuck!" said JoJo. "What a mess!"

Miss Winkle asked Farmer Jordan, "Where are the kids?"

Katie laughed. "Miss Winkle, we are right here!"

"I mean the baby goats," said Miss Winkle. "They are called kids."

"Oh!" said Katie. "I am learning a lot!"

"These kids are cool!" said Katie. "They jump and bounce around just like us!"

"Come and see my fields," said
Farmer Jordan. "I'm
growing corn for
popcorn."

"Yum!" yelled
Katie. "I love popcorn!
And I'm getting
hungry!"

Everybody sat down for lunch.
"I made these cupcakes," said Katie.
"They have eggs in them."

"Thank you for my eggs," Katie
called to the chickens.

Katie drank some milk. "Thank you for my milk," she called to the cows.

"It's time to go back to school,"
said Miss Winkle. "Please line up to
walk back to the bus."

"I am still hungry," said Katie. "I'd love some popcorn! The sun is so hot, the corn should be popping soon."

Katie walked into the cornfield.
"This row of corn is not popping," she
said. "I will go to the next row."

"This corn isn't popping either," sighed Katie. "I'd better go back." But the corn was so tall Katie couldn't find her way out!

"Oh, no!" Katie cried. "I'm lost."

Suddenly she heard, "Moo, Katie Woo! Moo, Katie Woo!" It was her class calling her!

Katie followed the sounds back to her class.

"I'm found!" She smiled. "Thank you for the moos!"

Katie told Farmer Jordan, "Something is wrong with your corn. It's not popping."

"I know," said Farmer Jordan. "That happens on your stove, not in the field."

"Oh," said Katie. "I know that now!"

On the way home, Katie said, "I would like to be a farmer."

"You just like the moos," teased JoJo.

"I do! I really do!" said Katie Woo.

Cooking with Katie Woo!

This project takes popcorn and makes it into corn on the cob. The recipe makes about 10 cobs. Ask a grown-up for help, and wash your hands to start!

What you need for the popcorn:

- 9 x 13 pan, sprayed with cooking spray
- wooden spoon
- 4 quarts popped popcorn
- 1 to 2 cups small colorful candies
- 6 tablespoons butter
- 5 cups mini marshmallows
- cooking spray

What you do:

1. Put popcorn in the baking dish. Mix in the candies.

2. Melt butter in a medium saucepan over low heat. Add the marshmallows and constantly stir with wooden spoon until melted.

3. Pour the marshmallow mix over popcorn mix, and stir to mix evenly. Let cool slightly. Spray your hands with cooking spray, then form the popcorn into corn-cob shapes. Now package them!

What you need for the package:

- small, narrow baggies with twist ties.
- strips of yellow tissue paper, measuring 6 inches wide and 15 inches long; and strips of green tissue paper, measuring 8 inches wide and 18 inches long
- 8-inch-long pieces of yellow or green ribbon

What you do:

1. Place each corn cob into a baggie. Secure with a twist tie. Wrap a strip of yellow paper around the baggie, covering the back but leaving the front showing. Repeat with a green strip of paper.

2. Twist the paper at the top of the baggie, so that it looks like a cob of corn. Tie a ribbon around the top.

Glamour Glasses

Katie Woo loves her blue glasses. They are stylish, and best of all, they help her see. You can make your own glasses using pipe cleaners. They won't change how you see, but they will give you a new look for some fashion fun!

What you need:

- 4 pipe cleaners
- ruler
- scissors
- a variety of small jewels, poms, or other decorations
- glue

What you do:

1. Using the ruler to measure, cut two pipe cleaners so they are 8 inches long.

2. Take one of the 8-inch pipe cleaners and form it into the shape of your choice. You could make a circle, heart, or square. Repeat with the other 8-inch pipe cleaner. These are the "lenses".

3. Take a third pipe cleaner and fold it in half. Twist the two halves together.

4. Use the twisted pipe cleaner to connect your "lenses". For best results wrap each end around the lenses 3-4 times.

5. Cut the last pipe cleaner in half. Twist each piece around the lense section to make the bows of the frame. Add a curve at the ends so the glasses fit around your ears.

6. Now you can decorate your glasses! Attach jewels, poms, or other small decorations with glue. Let dry.

About the Author

Fran Manushkin is the author of many popular picture books, including *Baby, Come Out!*; *Latkes and Applesauce: A Hanukkah Story*; *The Tushy Book; The Belly Book; and Big Girl Panties*. There is a real Katie Woo — she's Fran's great-niece — but she never gets in half the trouble of the Katie Woo in the books. Fran writes on her beloved Mac computer in New York City, without the help of her two naughty cats, Chaim and Goldy.

About the Illustrator

Tammie Lyon began her love for drawing at a young age while sitting at the kitchen table with her dad. She continued her love of art and eventually attended the Columbus College of Art and Design, where she earned a bachelors degree in fine art. After a brief career as a professional ballet dancer, she decided to devote herself full time to illustration. Today she lives with her husband, Lee, in Cincinnati, Ohio. Her dogs, Gus and Dudley, keep her company as she works in her studio.